LOVE EXIST

ISAAC NASH

For the Spirit of my first son Yousef.

My daughter's twin brother.

LOVE EXIST

Library of Congress Registration Number case # 1-10580212751

ISBN: 9798523661532 by KDP Amazon (Independently published)

Thanks

To my three Fathers, my heavenly Father and my Creator our Lord Jesus Christ, my biological Father Nabil Nashed, and my spiritual Father Yousef Halim. To my Lovely Mother Ansaf Yousef who loves me the most as I also do. To my sweetheart wife Sara and my lovely children Genesis, Daniel, and Jacob. To the first purchaser of my first book THE HEROK, Mr. G Thomas who both surprised and inspired me to move on. To my two countries, the one I was raised at where love exists and the one I live in where dreams come true when you act and work toward them with love.

LOVE EXIST

God creates me as a human being not something else great

Great is God's love to all human beings and the universe

Universe is full of greatness and most treasurable are the humans

Humans have everything love and hate require

Require yourself to be the first to love and never to hate

Hate no one because it is an option and you get to choose

Choose always to see people with the eyes of Love

Love Exist

Individual needs are plenty and they are not seen

Seen you may see. Open your eyes and your heart

Heart is shaped with the sign of love and maybe lost

Lost heart is found and it needs a rescue

Rescue some of your own now and continue with others

Others are waiting for you because you are the only one

One of you is here for you because she knows Love

Love Exist

Share something simple of yours with someone

Someone makes a great day of yours because of the conversation

Conversation leads to understanding and the possibility

Possibility takes place when we comprehend

Comprehend now not later because time is short

Short dialogue might be enough for now but not later

Later we will all share the talks of Love

Love Exist

The last piece may not complete the puzzle

Puzzle of many pieces may be completed even if it misses one

One piece of the puzzle is no longer with us and it is fine

Fine puzzle consist of pieces of love only

Only with love, every puzzle is possible

Possible and impossible puzzles are solvable by you

You may complete any puzzle ever with Love

Love Exist

LOVE EXIST

A ladder is leaning on a flag pole and it is cold now

Now you may use the ladder without any worries

Worries are scattered away because of what is hanging above

Above is for us all and we are proud of today and every day

Every day we salute it and it is our pride

Pride manifests inside us and is transferred out

Out there and up high is our flag of Love

Love Exist

Do you want to change or a change needs to occur

Occur and become too early

Early the time races me and wins

Wins they may achieve whether they love or not

Not everyone receives peoples' love but those who love

Love makes you change and you will change to love others

Others are your brothers and sisters who strive in Love

Love Exist

Many mistakes I have accomplished and none are the same

Same mistake was avoided because it belonged to someone else

Else and anymore they are the stepping stones for my strength

Strength develops along with the ways of attempts and errors

Errors are mostly mine and I am proud of

Of those who are mine, I have overcome with Love

Love Exist

All colors are favorites but one is for the one

One resembles love and it is red

Red may be a sign of love or blood

Blood is meant to keep our life flown by giving

Giving is much better than receiving and you will receive

Receive but do not ask and ask to give

Give for those who ask whether they deserve or not

Not today but now give with Love

Love Exist

LOVE EXIST

No sight but a heart and mind to believe

Believe everyone and follow no one

One of yours is the head of yours because he believes

Believes may lead to favorite or unpleasant thoughts

Thoughts are sometimes the flams of the upcoming fire

Fire is coming soon so be ready

Ready you are who does it right in Love

Love Exist

Time does not return or stop

Stop for a couple of seconds not minutes

Minutes have many seconds in which a victory is born

Born for the first time after years of trials

Trials are time-consuming but have passed like the wind

Wind wakes me up to see the victory of my team

Team is united in Love

Love Exist

I am limited. I know it. I am unlimited. I do not know it

It can be done not because I know it but believe in it

It is yours and belongs to us and none of us individually

Individually you may try but with them is better

Better things will happen if you labor and sleep less

Less time than you think is what you were looking for yesterday

Yesterday not yesteryear because you are fast

Fast is the behavior of yours of Love

Love Exist

Rain continues to drop every day

Every day is unique even if the rain stops

Stops are necessarily and they save lives

Lives of every small creature create our lives

Lives matters because they are individual hopes

Hopes of those little ones are the ultimate of Love

Love Exist

LOVE EXIST

It is rising and it is our pride

Pride belong to us all who live on the same land

Land of freedom and success

Success of happiness and the speed of the rebirth

Rebirth shine before us after a long time of battles

Battles are no longer here among us but our flag

Flag of one united nation on the same land of Love

Love Exist

Uncover yourself and be available

Available people have always less time

Time for actions and excitements

Excitements are a vital source of energy

Energy must be used very carefully and not to be wasted

Wasted time is lost hope of existence

Existence may not be if you do not Love

Love Exist

Parallels are many same lines but different colors

Colors may define who we are

Are you one of those lines in the graph?

Graph an organized path of saving yourself

Yourself is the light of others to believe

Believe that God exists

Exists are those who Love

Love Exist

Rolling the ball will never change its shape

Shape everything if you could and begin with yourself

Yourself is in front of the rest when it came to saving lives

Lives of those loved ones are very short

Short is always the time but the hope

Hope and pray for everyone to be saved

Saved people are so much grateful and they begin to Love

Love Exist

LOVE EXIST

Children may learn from your words and live by your actions

Actions show your family who you are

Are you leading your family or your family are still waiting?

Waiting in line is your child who needs your support

Support must take place if you want a strong nation

Nation is united by millions of small families

Families built-in Love

Love Exist

A mind is a huge library and should be open for everyone

Everyone seeks knowledge must receive it. Otherwise, he will die

Die now from every fault you have done and then wake up again

Again I am here believing in the rebirth of myself

Myself deserves to love me but others more

More than millions of times I am reborn again

Again and again, I will see everyone with Love

Love Exist

Words are many and they show no sign

Sign of love resembles simplicity

Simplicity should never be when it comes to actions

Actions require sincerity and courage

Courage to plant, face the weather, then reap

Reap only what is yours then give it all away

Away you are not because you belong to everyone

Everyone loves you because you have and give Love

Love Exist

Assurance is not guaranteed because nothing is

Is it because of you or me it does not matter but for us

Us are all here today so thank you, dear Lord

Lord of hosts is among us and it is certain and secured

Secured deeds are your reputation among nations

Nations are separated because of the absence of Love

Love Exist

LOVE EXIST

Thirteen may not be your favorite number so choose one

One number or set of numbers may make you a millionaire

Millionaire or millionaires are your siblings

Siblings have different parents but the same heart

Heart beats to beat the impossible and the possible

Possible things may be impossible for others somewhere

Somewhere else they are waiting for your Love

Love Exist

Store or reserve nothing because it will vanish soon

Soon you will observe it like every individual body

Body will be but the soul

Soul of an individual may return to its original

Original people may survive forever on earth and after earth

Earth is just a platform. It is not our home

Home of those who Love

Love Exist

Celebrate the birthday of someone every day

Every day is the birthday of millions

Millions of people are your harvest but someone

Someone still lives in darkness and still waiting for you

You save others. You save yourself

Yourself is the water of those millions of people

People may learn faster if they first learn to Love

Love Exist

Allow tears to occur but not to last

Last thing to think of is what you do next if you win

Win fast to allow others to win also before they die

Die for others to show the importance of their lives

Lives are too many but few will be saved

Saved people are so much appreciated but sometimes they forget

Forget, forgive, and Love

Love Exist

LOVE EXIST

A new era is happening right now because of your deeds

Deeds are small seeds that grow trees of faith

Faith saved my brothers from death and gave me another chance

Chance to survive and allow others to breathe

Breathe the air of the new era because it is here already

Already a victory is taken place and it is for us all

All of us will overcome and survive only if we Love

Love Exist

Joint bones are meant to be

Be everywhere possible and if you cannot do not stop

Stop not because the clock does not

Not only you here living and the land for us all

All are the same but different are thought and believes

Believes leads and faith saves

Saves are many lives whom they had faith in Love

Loves Exist

Feel the heat with your bare feet

Feet of love is much better than a mile of hate

Hate no one even if they hate you so much

Much of us are in pain and it is secondly routine

Routine becomes the foundation of our upcoming success

Success happens because we Love

Love Exist

Skating is not for everyone even with two legs

Legs lead to more legs after the two prints

Prints are not meant to last like everything else

Else and many more different and new people are coming

Coming to you a new friendship so be careful

Careful people are too slow sometimes

Sometimes you wish to speed up but can not

Not later. Do not postpone Love

Love Exist

LOVE EXIST

They were part of the process of me and my siblings

Siblings need everything possible in life especially their parents

Parents are almost the source of everything to their children

Children are shinning to the world of possibilities

Possibilities become reality as I was born

Born in the family of wisdom and faith of my parents

Parents build a strong generation because they do have Love

Love Exist

I never wanted to be here because I do not belong

Belong to someplace else I do not know or see

See what is unseen might be my rescue

Rescue is my proposed right that many others are looking for

For whether we like it or not no one is leaving here

Here we must live together

Together we must be and we can make it only with Love

Love Exist

A letter has been sent to you

You may or may not read it or know about it

It belongs to you and only you

You may stay where you are and I am coming near

Near and even closer is the time for us to meet

Meet no one please and wait for me. I am on my way

Way or no way at all I will come because you are my Love

Love Exist

Old days are new but just a few

Few people can recall the few special days

Days made me feel nothing but all hope and desire

Desire to live not only like those past ones but better

Better than ever is coming forever

Forever special days will last even after we are gone

Gone are those who had no Love

Love Exist

LOVE EXIST

I am not who I am

Am I able to cross this hurricane?

Hurricane is made to terminate us all

All we can do is nothing at all. No, it is not true

True people appear in difficulties and hardships

Hardships are born to make us born

Born a new friendship in Love

Love Exist

She runs faster than herself without a pause

Pause not to listen to those who never move on

On her shoulders a very heavy burden

Burden may burn off anyone but her

Her unique scent spreads out too fast like her speed

Speed up without a return. At your back are failures

Failures are waiting desperately for her. She has Love

Love Exist

We are too many but not together

Together we have a strength of a mountain

A mountain full of rocks is underneath many lives

Lives of those who belong to us and generations to come

Come to your loved ones and remain for some time

Time is too short being together

Together we are an example of Love

Love Exist

Walk on the road now then speed up later when you see the light

Light will appear to those who strive for it

It will come to you more abundantly if you have love

Love everyone and everything possible along the way

Way or ways it does not matter as long as you are alive

Alive are those who see others and offer them services

Services you provide spread more Love

Love Exist

LOVE EXIST

I am sorry for what I have done to you

You are me and I belong to you. Please forgive

Forgive and do not forget where we came from

From where we have met first we were born again

Again, I am sorry and it will never happen again

Again, nothing I can do in my life because you are not here

Here in our place, I am waiting for you with my Love

Love Exist

Water in the pond does not shake under the Tornado

Tornado has shattered and demolished everything

Everything is possible even under the Tornado

Tornado has no mercy for those who had no mercy

Mercy is granted to the creatures under the water in the pond

The pond is near and unseen but saved

Saved we are because our water's Love

Love Exist

Distance between us means one day

Day and night pass first then I and the morning follow next

Next to me is your patience and next to you is mine

Mine and all of me is yours

Yours is the love of myself and my fellows

Fellows were born and raised on your land

Land of yours means hope, future, and Love

Love Exist

I hear about you from my friends in school

School is the place I develop socially hear about you

You were there one day but not today nor tomorrow

Tomorrow and every day I need you

You probably see and hear me now

Now, I live with others because you are not here

Here I wish you were because I miss your Love

Love Exist

LOVE EXIST

A flower in my hand is full of thorns

Thorns are for me and the flower is yours

Yours is everything that belongs to me. Please know this

This flower will never die simply because it sprung up in love

Love is the continuous nourishment for you and the flower

Flower of course is red to keep your heart alive

Alive are us three. You, me, and Love

Love Exist

Some people fell in the pit without a rescue

Rescue may not come at all but do not be afraid

Afraid is a word that may destroy you if it passes your mind

Mind is stronger than the whole body

Body of yours is not yours so do not worry

Worry about others more than yourself even in difficult times

Times of liberation is coming near because you had Love

Love Exist

Please start and do not worry if you succeed or not

Not only you may win but you may have a superior winning

Winning requires everything of you even to the last breath

Breath is in you and others but yours is different and unique

Unique people are all of us and that's how we were created

Created nature belongs to God

God is the source of Love

Love Exist

Two thousand words are not enough

Enough talks and it is time to either write, dance, or sleep

Sleep less. Only you can do it if you have a vision in life

Life is shorter every day after another

Another word is needed to make a meaningful message

Message all of them even if some have no ears

Ears only hear those who Love

Love Exist

LOVE EXIST

Barriers divide lands and nations but not people

People live together and are united

United people are nations and generations

Generations write the history of generations to come

Come and observe the power of bonds

Bonds and oaths are established by us always

Always what ties us is Love

Love Exist

Lean your head on the below without any fears

Fears are approaching those who speak loud

Loud voices lead to nowhere but voice pain

Pain of having done nothing to others. Or

Or doing too many things without others love

Love is magical and gains no pain but happiness

Happiness is all that you will get if you Love

Love Exist

I am not sure if my current status

Status of temptations and invitations

Invitations to join the celebration of the uncertain

Uncertain people get lost and fall easily

Easily you have arrived and easily you are leaving

Leaving what you have not finished is not cool

Cool and certain you are regardless of your age

Age is not a number but the experience of Love

Love Exist

Whether you come to me or I will fasten to come to you

You are not the only thing I want in life but important

Important is to know who you are but not all the times

Times will come where you will discover someone else inside you

You are not what you were because you will never be tomorrow

Tomorrow is undefined. Be ready to Love

Love Exist

LOVE EXIST

Decorate your home with less furniture and more love

Love your family and teach them how to love one another

Another person will join our family soon

Soon or later people will discover if you love them or not

Not everyone talks about love loves but you

You love. You know it. Just do more of it

It deserves your Love

Love Exist

Save some money and go somewhere else new

New places will show you different kind of love

Love is everywhere but here is better

Better because I can show you it is unlimited

Unlimited people know there is no end to their love

Love may sound different but it is the same

Same people. Different places. Same Love

Love Exist

Underneath the oceans are dolphins and many more

More creates underwater strive to survive without compassion

Compassion does not exist and maybe some kindness

Kindness leads to love as dolphins do

Do it with love and feel better

Better than anything are your actions

Actions come afterthoughts and before Love

Love Exist

Do not teach children. Let them learn from you

You learn from children more while teaching them less

Less time spent with children is enough to teach you something

Something is unbroken and breakable like children

Children have purity like Heaven but not earth

Earth is very cheap comparing to Heaven

Heaven where everything magnificent is like Love

Love Exist

LOVE EXIST

Save those rare moments

Moments are another moments for us and many more

More moments are not guaranteed because nothing is

Is he or she are worth those moments?

Moments of laughs deserve remembrance for more laughs

Laughs heal hearts and souls

Souls provide other souls with Love

Love Exist

I saw my whole past life in one dream as a sequence of events

Events I still carry in the back of my mind

Mind of beautiful things is vigorous

Vigorous people are always givers

Givers give any time and a lot of times

Times of giving are the best times for the giver

The giver gives everything he or she has with Love

Love Exist

On the same bus, everyone had a spot

Spot for an individual may be available later for another

Another person is coming to take over and that is life

Life does not last on earth and was not created to last

Last thing you think of is yourself. Your self also needs you

You are the person who never came and will never come again

Again you still here. You may last if you do it with Love

Love Exist

Knees are used for mobility and humility

Humility means meekness of strength

Strength is rising among us by our youngest

Youngest people have the power to move a mountain

A mountain is in the midst of us for security and protection

Protection does not exist in many places and regions

Regions need you now than ever. Please offer your Love

Love Exist

LOVE EXIST

Every shape has a beginning and an end

End some habits of you which allow others not seeing you

You may be present and unseen at all

All you can do is to smile love

Love will come to you faster than you ever imagined

Imagined thoughts are not true but Love

Love Exist

Everything was lost gradually. I am here alone

Alone those who have love but never exercise it

It takes courage sometimes to love

Love from your heart not just from outside

Outside might be the only way out

Out there, many look after your love

Love gradually, then do not stop

Stop anything in life but Love

Love Exist

Two hands make a difference for many open hands

Hands stretch up high to their Creator

Creator loves you

You may follow no one but Him who loves you

You fill up some of those opened hand at you capacity

Capacity of you will increases because you give and Love

Love Exist

One thousand four hundred-forty minutes in a day

A day is today. How many minutes are left?

Left minutes matters. Each one has sixty seconds

Seconds of true love institute millions of lives

Lives lead to lives lead to more lives

Lives are ours and theirs

Theirs are the hope for more lives

Lives matters for those who Love

Love Exist

LOVE EXIST

If you never planted a seed it is all fine. Try

Try to love someone from your heart for a long time

Time passed of loving someone is not wasted but invested

Invested love is the best seed to plant

Plant a seed of love when possible to make the impossible

Impossible things are never impossible if you have Love

Love Exist

What is the name of your love?

Love has many names and yours must be the pure love

Love, think, act, behave, work, give, and dream in purity

Purity is the simple key to open all doors

Doors locked are unlocked for those who have pure love

Love is love and should not be mingled with something else

Else and more to come my love to you my dear friends

Friends know how to be friends because they know how to love

Love Exist

Sons and daughters never lost their mother

Mother of many not just ours

Ours is the mother who sacrificed her whole life for us

Us and many more owe her everything

Everything was taught and given to us through her

Her is the Kingdom of Heaven because she deserves it

It belongs to her and maybe us if we also do it in Love

Love Exist

I sing and dance outside and my umbrella in the heat of the day

Day of yours you may adore while others may marvel

Marvel not to see me singing and dancing under the heat

Heat and even more heat I do not feel or recognize

Recognize yourself what is write and what is wrong

Wrong steps may lead to devastations

Devastations may be avoided if you have Love

Love Exist

LOVE EXIST

Knockdown the walls and install many windows

Windows bring light and love instead

Instead of keeping it dark, light it up

Up in Heaven are the source of light. Pray for more

More light to come for the sons of light

Light through windows lights our home and life

Life of my family through the light of Love

Love Exist

I feel powerless and it is a shame

Shame on me and lonely I am

Am I able to continue like this? I do not think so

So many people around me and though I am alone

Alone I am and for a long time

Time has passed and I am the same

Same lonely people have something mutual. They do not Love

Love Exist

Expect children to do what adults often do not do

Do it in a very simple way with a lot of imagination

Imagination is among the few unlimited things in life

Life needs you to imagine and live the unreal for some times

Times of the unusual is fun, fast, and non-repeatable

Non-repeatable is every single second

Second with you is your Love

Love Exist

Take a break, think, meditate, and smile

Smile to your heart and wait for the result

Result of what is seen soon

Soon your heart will rejoice and you have a duty

A duty to make someone else's heart rejoices

Rejoices is happening among those who a heart

Heart celebrate others' amusements with Love

Love Exist

LOVE EXIST

Working under pressure becomes a life routine

Routine is an amendment and is capable of a change

Change it now and if it not possible try to reduce it

It is very challenging to make a change sometimes

Sometimes people pray and act for the change

Change may not change and there will be no change

Change may easily happen if you have Love

Love Exist

Go sit on the seashore and do not look back

Back are all that you do and you need to rest

Rest for some time but not a long time

Time to mind some times and to breathe instead

Instead of sitting you could walk and/or run

Run fast if you can with your friend

Friend is at your side because he has Love

Love Exist

A fish is closed its mouth is difficult to catch

Catch your mouth before judging someone

Someone loves you because of an unknown intention

Intention is needed to those who love you or not

Not everyone feels ready at all times

Times are perplexing sometimes and you need to talk

Talk about everything and everyone with Love

Love Exist

God is the source of everything you imagine and do not imagine

Imagine God loves you and you love God

God loves you love each one including your enemies

Enemies are in your life for a purpose

Purpose to forgive and love to be forgiven and loved

Loved people are never forgiven

Forgiven people still have a chance to give people Love

Love Exist

LOVE EXIST

In some cases some hearts are diamonds

Diamonds are rare and tough to find

Find your heart. It is your diamond

Diamonds are made through clarity, purity, and love

Love makes it possible for clarity and purity

Purity and clarity are established and founded through Love

Love Exist

Most things in life could be sold and purchased but love

Love must be free through giving and services

Services return to you and your generations in many forms

Forms are not formed but are naturally happening

Happening and showing others its possibilities

Possibilities of thanksgiving

Thanksgiving is a selected practice

Practice to give Love

Love Exist

The five of us are no longer five tomorrow

Tomorrow one of us is leaving and we do not know who

Who will leave us does matter because we will miss him or her

Her entire life was a perfect example like him and the rest of us

Us and all of us are one unity and we do not want to be separated

Separated people are not happy individuals

Individuals are all here now with one thing in common. Love

Love Exist

Fences and boundaries I have built throughout the years

Years have passed and I cannot change but be worse

Worse occasion is the same as the best. They all the same

The same is my life and I need help

Help is out there and everywhere. Just try and it is ok

Ok to fall a million times as long as you are trying

Trying it with love is much easier. Thus, Love

Love Exist

LOVE EXIST

Have patience with those who are different from you

You are the only one who wants it this way

Way or ways it does not matter. Let it go

Go and observe how others do it and then chose

Chose what is suitable for you and it does not have to be perfect

Perfect is no one of us. Have patience

Patience is an element of Love

Love Exist

If you have extra do not waste it or restore it

It may be shared with your brothers and sisters on earth

Earth is full of people whom their life will be better if

If help them out and supply them just with some of their needs

Needs may be simple to you but everything to them now

Now you will have a pleasant life full of happiness

Happiness and mercy for those who serve in Love

Love Exist

Stocks and real estates have added me a fortune

Fortune helps my whole family to live better

Better home and lifestyle

Lifestyle your life to live healthier

Healthier life is given to us all if we share

Share some of your wealth or fortune and gain more

More is given to those who invest in Love

Love Exist

Five miles out of ten thousand miles is a progress

Progress enables you to get closer to your goals

Goals and visions are approaching you faster than you imagined

Imagined ten thousand miles could end up approaching even more

More than you think or you do not think about will happen to you

You are among the few who will advance beyond

Beyond your goals and visions, you will obtain if you have Love

Love Exist

LOVE EXIST

Whether you like music or not it creates moods

Moods of special moments with those loved ones

Ones are sometimes few or rare. Music compensates your friends

Friends are never compensated. Find more

More people are accompanied together but never friends

Friends are those who need nothing from you but you

You are a true friend because you have given Love

Love Exist

Hear your words as you speak to congregations

Congregations hear you but do not listen to you

You try hard to make changes but never happened

Happened to pass none of your words

Words meant to change the rest of us and always

Always have patience if you want to be one of the advisors

Advisors advise people have something in common. Love

Love Exist

Next time you meet try to reconcile

Reconcile because you may not see each other again

Again, do not listen to your mind but your heart

Heart can forgive and forget

Forget those who trespass against you and feel better

Better is to have no enemies at all but friends

Friends are rare to find. They do exist somewhere at a certain time

Time to reconcile with Love

Love Exist

Choose between understanding people or yourself

Yourself is hard to understand as well as people

People are not different to be similar

Similar or identical two do not exist

Exist are millions of million different people

People are always looking for someone to exchange Love

Love Exist

LOVE EXIST

She likes to fish but not fishes

Fishes are under and above the water but live in the water

Water is a source of life for those under and above

Above and under she needs to learn how to fish!

Fish for every possible opportunity to make your dreams alive

Alive she is but not her dreams yet

Yet and soon her dreams are no longer dreams because she Loves

Loves Exist

Time is either super-fast or too slow

Slow down on your judgment and hesitate

Hesitate before you crack someone else's with your words

Words must be kind regardless. Believe it. Regardless

Regardless of your short times, give some to someone

Someone may or may not appreciates the time you give

Give regardless. One thing makes it possible. Love

Love Exist

Sugar and honey are not the same

Same desire most people look for. Happiness

Happiness is temporary but repeats

Repeats are those beautiful red and white roses

Roses are the seed of love

Love may be expressed in your way or ways

Ways and paths are plenty to show your Love

Love Exist

I cannot get in because all doors are locked

Locked doors are locked and will never be opened

Opened doors are no longer available

Available light only and behind locked doors

Doors are neat and organized next to many other doors

Doors are almost walls

Walls do not exist in the presence of Love

Love Exist

LOVE EXIST

He makes me laugh but selfish and dishonest

Dishonest and selfish I am. Just like him. We must separate

Separate to find someone else to teach me otherwise

Otherwise, we will collapse and fight

Fight with no one but let it go

Go and find love

Love will teach you everything. Learn to Love

Love Exist

My ears are still on my shoulders and cannot take them off

Off my shoulders are nothing but many more are still on

On me are many burdens. They slow me down

Down the shore might be my relief and discharge

Discharge one at a time and do not catch any more

More are still coming. All up to you

You may release them all together by Love

Love Exist

Stand up even if you do not have two legs

Legs are not necessarily to stand up and to speed up

Up in Heaven, someone is watching and you have heard of Him

Him and only through Him you may rise. Believe it

It has happened with many others. Why not you!

You do your part and keep the rest to Him

Him and only through Him is Love

Love Exist

Exchange but do not receive now. Wait

Wait for your descendants to receive

Receive what you deserve and less. Keep the rest later

Later, you will have clear observation and you will be able to see

See like those who do not have eyes because they see better

Better not to know the best time to receive. It is like a surprise

Surprise your descendants with your reputation of Love

Love Exist

LOVE EXIST

Morphology is the study of words

Words may express what you as a person has gone through

Through many impediments and complications, a person is born

Born yesterday but today is completely different

Different because he was loved and cured

Cured of every evil and hardness of hearts and minds

Minds lead us to either hate or Love

Love Exist

Above the ground, everything was and never returned back

Back in time somethings were the same

Same of today will never happen because it never happened

Happened smiles are me, them, and over there

There will be what is above and underground

Underground holds unknown fathers and mothers

Mothers taught their children everything possible with Love

Love Exist

Rainbow is known for its magnificent sky appearance

Appearance of many look magnificent but only from outside

Outside are some of us and the rest are sleeping

Sleeping babes are in Heaven

Heaven is ready for those who are ready

Ready you are because you have given all that you have

Have a nice day my dear. Sincerely, Love

Love Exist

It is cold inside but very hot outside

Outside no one can survive. How come you are?

Are you like us or somehow different?

Different people may show you what survival is

Is she the daughter of the corner baker?

Backer has taught her daughter to sweeten her love

Love is very sweet and never harms you. Again sweet Love

Love Exist

LOVE EXIST

No one will allow you to step in. They say you do not belong

Belong to anywhere you want to and do not give up

Up and down your life is but you probably will rest in between

Between those small words of yours is who you are

Are you afraid of trying? Or are you lazy?

Lazy people like to sit down. Do not do that

That door is where my entrance will be and I believe it

It can be done even if it never happened before

Before you are too many but you will enter by Love

Love Exist

The sound of the waving flag is heard through the wind

The wind is the pride of us all

All trees are standing by for protection

Protection comes from underground and is solid

Solid is he who knows how to use Love

Love Exist

I hear too many noes but yeses

Yeses are rare to hear. Try to provide them

Them and through them, people believe in themselves and improve

Improve what seems impossible

Impossible to live your whole life without any love

Love people and if you cannot find them, love anything instead

Instead of waiting, act, and act very quickly

Quickly find someone or something to Love

Love Exist

Plus or minus is always my bank account

Account what makes true values of life

Life without values is life without values

Values remain forever and establish new ones

Ones are coming. Try to be involved

Involved people not necessarily have Love

Love Exist

LOVE EXIST

I can or I cannot it does not matter

Matter things do not matter

Matter is what you do for your next step or steps to come

Come and learn from others but follow your steps

Steps of yours are unique and they do matter

Matter is what makes people improve and save

Save some steps for others because you must have Love

Love Exist

If I compare my life with yours then I should be grateful

Grateful to ask for forgiveness and nothing else

Else I have to pray and be thankful for everything

Everything is possible to those who fear God

God has given you more than a nation has received

Received gifts are not free

Free you are if you fear God and give Him Love

Love Exist

Do not just believe in yourself because someone says so

So, you need to learn, labor, strive, commit, obligate, and resume

Resume even if you know there is no winning

Winning will come when you do not know as the wind

The wind is not everywhere. Just many places

Places are full of those who deserve winds

Winds are faster for those who obtained Love

 Love Exist

Take a picture of those who are close to you to see yourself

Yourself can be improved always to be enhanced

Enhanced souls are the soils of developments of many

Many are limited but capable and have a passion to change

Change yourself not others and have them watch you

You may make a difference if you have changed

Changed people should maintain it with Love

Love Exist

LOVE EXIST

I called on you because you are my only rescue

Rescue me and I will serve you forever and ever

Ever I will leave you. Please give me a chance

Chance to repent and correct my past for my future

Future is all for you and about you my Father

Father and savior of everyone including myself

Myself does not deserve but calling on your Love

Love Exist

It has been raining for a long time without a stop

Stop grumbling for what other nations do not have

Have you seen how others are living?

Living is the ultimate purpose for millions of our brothers

Brothers have responsibilities to care for and share

Share anything if possible for those who live the impossible

Impossible for you to hear about this and do not offer Love

Love Exist

Happy birthday to you

You truly are born today. We are proud of you

You succeeded to prove it to us and the world

The world of possibilities exists

Exists are those butterflies who have struggled for the shape

Shape yourself for what make yourself and others to be proud

Proud you are and proud we have

Have fun and enjoy your times with Love

Love Exist

My doctor said "I will not make it to Christmas"

Christmas is very near. I do not want to go

Go pray and thank God that you know the time

Time to go is unknown for all of us but very few

Few people are blessed to know the time of their departure

Departure will be for everyone without exception. Give Love

Love Exist

LOVE EXIST

A single, a separated, or a married person, they all the same

The same human being who must live on earth to face tribulations

Tribulation is made for humans without any exceptions

Exceptions do not exist but exist even more for those who love

Love regardless of your extreme conditions. Resume your battle

Battle will end son and you are among the winners

Winners were not born to be winners but they decided to be

Be the winner who knows that he has won because he had Love

Love Exist

Take off your shoes and touch the ground

The ground is very cold. Can you feel it for a couple of seconds?

Seconds of your is nothing comparing to other years

Years have passed and my feet never knew what a shoe is

Is it possible for me to do something about it?

It depends on you. Do not wait to provide Love

Love Exist

One thing at a time and do not catch the wind

The wind is full of many duties that come together at once

Once upon a time, I was able to manage it

It belongs to me. I have to face it and deal with it

It does not matter how long it takes me to finish it

It will be done. One thing at a time

Time to celebrate your accomplishments with those you Love

Love Exist

I cannot stop judging others

Others do not know that I talk about them. Why Do I do it?

It hearts if someone knew about it

It hearts more the person who does the judgment

Judgment is useless and makes no sense at all

All my judgments will return to me some days

Days will come when I stop judging only if I have true Love

Love Exist

LOVE EXIST

I have no idea about my existence but my parents do

Do you realize how much they love you?

You are both of them in one shape of you

You are here with them. Do not be afraid or worried

Worried are those who do not have parents

Parents institute almost everything for their child

Child is feeling secure all his life because his parents' Love

Love Exist

We have communicated for almost a decade and still do not get it

It is never about the time but the harmony

Harmony is either found or not found at all forever

Forever we may be together but not together

Together we have to make it happen because we understand

Understand each other's weaknesses and strengths

Strengths are found in Love

Love Exist

A talent God has given me and still, I do not know

Know and discover yourself along the way

Way or another you must exist and be born again

Again, some people are born and gone and do not know

Know and discover yourself before you leave

Leave something beneficent for others to use and to remember you

You cannot discover anything if you do not have Love

Love Exist

Plenty of different successes exist. The most are peoples' love

Love people so that they love you back

Back of your mind is pride. Erase it

It does not matter who you are. What matter who you love

Love to give and give to be loved

Loved people are both happy and successful

Successful is the person who knows Love

Love Exist

LOVE EXIST

My prediction is fifty-fifty. Maybe a boy or a girl

Girl of the day is the happiness of tomorrow

Tomorrow it might be the boy of our future

Future your life on neither a boy nor a girl but a great human

Human is not complicated but simple as a dove

Dove on the top of the building is watching what happens below

Below this surface, no one knows but some men and women

Women make generations of those who Love

Love Exist

I am looking at you without a pause

Pause not if you do the right thing and harm no one

One day God will reward you because you labored

Labored and tired you are now but later

Later you will find rest with those who had labored

Labored people do not feel it because they labor in Love

Love Exist

My daddy's shoulder is the best seat in the house

House is too small in space but huge of hugs and kisses

Kisses are plenty. My mom gives us a lot of them every day

Every day I am on my daddy's shoulder and my sister laughs

Laughs are the sounds of our house in and out

Out there are different world but we are not afraid

Afraid is a word that my parents never mentioned but Love

Love Exist

Money produces temporary money but love produces lasting love

Love as much as possible and be ready to be inspired

Inspired people inspire others especially those who are close

Close to you is the sound of hope

Hope the wealth and fortune that come from love

Love is free but its rewards are priceless

Priceless is your love to me. Thanks for your Love

Love Exist

LOVE EXIST

Little love does count love

Love and feel its feeling. It is joy, delight, and many more

More to come to you and your generations

Generations have missed love and cannot come back

Back in time, there was the same love

Love may have some generations to remain for legacy

Legacy is made through Love

Love Exist

You are weaker than you believe. Stronger than you do not believe

 Believe that one day you are powerless and it is up to your deeds

Deeds deliver you to everlasting life or no life at all

All your strength is not yet discovered. Find More

More inside and outside of you work out together to make you

You may strive less in case you have much love

Love makes everything much simpler for anyone who has Love

Love Exist

The system is not made for you and the remaining

The remaining are all outside of here. There is no system

 System is rare and we have to get out of here

Here is everything corrupt and we are helpless

Helpless are you. There is a liberation

Liberation is happening through love

Love? Does not belong here

Here and everywhere you can launch Love

Love Exist

You may choose any path you want but I will love you forever

Forever you are inside my mind, soul, heart, and everything else

Else and ever more you are the one and the only one

One day you have entered inside me and that was it

It is the best thing that has happened and will happen in my life

Life without you is not life. I will give all my Love

Love Exist

LOVE EXIST

Famous I am but never loved. Loved you are with fame

Fame with love is the desire of anyone

Anyone can be loved for one simple condition. Love

Love like a baby loves his mother

Mother is the source of love. Sometimes

Sometimes you love and you do not get it. It is ok

Ok to live to love even if you do not get back Love

Love Exist

I spent the whole night on that day crying

Crying has taught me not to regret and forget

Forget who forgot you. Love him or her and move on

On and on I will be and become

Become someone who loves everyone and anyone regardless

Regardless of anything that has happened or coming to happen

Happen to become my existence to give always Love

Love Exist

God, please help me to love you

You are my Father, Mother, Brother, and Sister

Sister has taught her brother the existence of God

God created everything and is everything

Everything has a beginning, middle, and end. All have love

Love God from your heart, mind, soul, and all your strength

Strength comes by and from Love

Love Exist

I stand before you today like any other day

Day after a day I am the same and never seeing any improvement

Improvement happens to some people but myself

Myself needs to see a different person tomorrow the next time

Time to change when I stand again before you

You cannot do anything for me. I know it

It is up to me if I can Love

Love Exist

LOVE EXIST

Hymns and songs are heard next door

Door stands between us. Can someone open it?

It has been closed for a long time. I am tired

Tired are those who never tasted any source of love

Love is there. I see it but cannot feel it

It belongs to some people and not all

All can love but few can Love

Love Exist

I never knew you had loved me or you do

Do you mean me? Are you sure?

Sure I can but not ready yet. Need some time

Time is not enough. We need every second together

Together we will live happily and make the rest happy as well

Well, let us try and give each other a chance

A chance is not welcome but your Love

Love Exist

All the words have been said and they are not enough for you

You deserve what any other person has ever got

Got everything in life because I got you

You are the love and the love is you

You are mine now and myself is yours forever

Forever will be ours

Ours is Love

Love Exist

Insist to love even if everyone around hates

Hates destroys the person before anybody else

Elsewhere hates to exist but do not remain

Remain calm. Let it go. Resume your speed faster than a train

Train your brain to have self-control

Self-control is not a gift. It can be gained

Gained are the reputations of Love

Love Exist

LOVE EXIST

Obedient and polite my daughter is

Is there anyone like her? Plenty

Plenty of mothers have shown excellence in raising their daughters

Daughters are the future of our land

Land of magic and imagination

Imagination has traveled beyond anything else but Love

Love Exist

Send the same message of love to many people

People will respond differently

Differently, because we are the same and different

Different responses do not change your love toward all of them

Them and the rest are your responsibility to love

Love and benefits correlate and always connect

Connect with as many people as possible with passion

Passion to love is the best of Love

Love Exist

My father taught me to smile when greeting others

Others smile back and some seem to wonder

Wondering if in the dictionary of love

Love was in our house and thanks to our father

Father is the number one father of everyone not just his children

Children are proud of their adoring and caring father

Father of all is the father of Love

Love Exist

I never knew that love existed until I met you

You opened my eyes and it will never be closed

Closed-minded are those who limit their love

Love should be unlimited

Unlimited roads of successes and prosperity

Prosperity is born when your love is and become

Become a man who allows people to Love

Love Exist

LOVE EXIST

Love of yesterday is history. Today is the history of love

Love is every day and is unlike any other day

Day of no love does not count. How many do you have?

Have patience with those who do not have love

Love is born and is given always for free

Free I give you my love and I am waiting for nothing in return

Return to your loved ones soon because they give Love

Love Exist

My life is yours

Yours is another chance to live and to correct everything

Everything is possible as long as you have a life

Life is restored now. Make use of it

It might be the only and last opportunity for you

You live it right because it is mine and I want it to be right

Right now I am gone. My life is your forever by Love

Love Exist

Love is mercy. Mercy is love

Love is giving. Giving is love

Love is forgiveness. Forgiveness is love

Love is service. Service is love

Love is light. Light is love

Love is marriage. Marriage is Love

Love Exist

My father decides to give up his second job for me and my brother

Brother and sister now have time to spend with their father

Father gives time to his children. It is love and investment

Investment in children is the best

Best of yours is given to them and they deserve it

It sends many massages and teaches many lessons

Lesson are taught daily by my father

Father gives out everything happily in Love

Love Exist

LOVE EXIST

I do not have to promise you. My words are sincere

Sincere is the man who fulfills his words

Words of a man come out of a man or a woman

A woman is sincere and is responsible

Responsible is he or she who stand up for what is right

Right now I am looking at you with a pride

Pride is given to me by him or her in Love

Love Exist

She holds the brush and colors his drawing

Drawing was done by him and never was completed

Completed by her because he has gone

Gone to leave it up to her to finish it

It is the drawing of her heart inside his heart

Heart is drawing inside another's heart becomes one heart

Heart beats another heart in Love

Love Exist

Many leaves are still attached to the same branch in the fall

Fall season means all leave is withered away and are fallen down

Down on the ground are all the leaves except some

Some leaves are still up there holding tied

Tied is their unity and it may last

Last year was the year of their spring and it might be this year also

Also and many more days to come together

Together we will be because we have Love

Love Exist

Expect enemies if you decide to give love

Love will gain some enemies but plenty of loves

Loves beats anything and everything even enemies

Enemies do not last and vanished quickly

Quickly they come and quickly they leave. Do not pay attention

Attention should be given to everyone in Love

Love Exist

LOVE EXIST

No one is perfect except God

God can make you perfect if he wants. He wants you

You give yourself to God and you will be perfect

Perfect is God's love toward humans

Humans do not understand how they were created

Created are every one of us for a purpose

Purpose to live and serve who created you

You know this and offer your Love

Love Exist

She has both family and success. I am jealous

Jealous she is because love does not exist

Exist and inject some love inside you to remove the jealousy out

Out of you is everything that may harm you before anyone else

Else and more time is given to look at the bright side

Side by side you should be and become with Love

Love Exist

Elegant and handsome my husband is

Is he ever cared about anyone but himself?

Himself is first then comes anyone else after

After today I and the kids cannot take it anymore

Anymore but more chances were given to him to change

Change cannot be made in his case. We still love him

Him we are worried about but him about us

Us we will try it again this time. We will give him more Love

Love Exist

Roots above ground not under

Underground are hidden resources and treasures

Treasure is everywhere. The most are inside your heart

Heart knows how to be kind and give love

Love creates deep roots inside others' hearts

Hearts and more hearts distribute Love

Love Exist

LOVE EXIST

Open a book, read it, enjoy it, and think about its message

Message is meant to be used to improve your life

Life is short. Do not waste it on unnecessary mistakes

Mistakes may be avoided if you had prior knowledge

Knowledge is out there. Some are in books

Books are opened to open some doors and keep some closed

Closed books are waiting for you to teach you Love

Love Exist

Kids of all ages play in the park

Park embraces all kinds of us as one family

Family of many individuals shares one or two goals

Goals of playing and socializing for some time

Time for fun is not wasted and fills up your tank

Tank of patience, endurance, tolerance, strength, survival, and love

Love for others to Love

Love Exist

My grandfather taught me to plant a tree

Tree witnesses the love between us and maybe more

More lands are given for more trees

Trees are offering some shades for some love

Love is written on the tree for remembrance

Remembrance proofs the history of love

Love to plant a seed to become a tree to witness Love

Love Exist

The sun rises on the good and the bad but somewhere

Somewhere needs the sun for life

Life is there and everyone is taking a share

Share what you may not need with those who may need

Need to survive because I belong

Belong to you is sunshine

Sunshine is a symbol of Love

Love Exist

LOVE EXIST

The food was delicious as well as the company

Company with best and new friends

Friends are all gone except me and the bill

Bill is mine because it is my turn this time

Time did not pass until it was all paid off

Paid off by someone who decided to express his kindness

Kindness is Love

Love Exist

You have a letter delivered to your house today

Today my life was restored to me by a letter

Letter from a son. They will meet soon

Soon, a son and a father will meet after more than a decade

A decade of broken hearts

Hearts back to life

Life needs Love

Love Exist

I want to live and I need to be loved

Loved people are happy

Happy you are if you have some people to love you

You live without worries with open arms to the world

The world offers no love and it is miserable

Miserable are those regions of stricken routine only

Only love can change everything to be better

Better is every next day of your Love

Love Exist

My mother told me if you love you win and never loose

Loose body's weight and mind's negative weight

Weight is on your friends' shoulders. You may help out

Out of the ordinary, you are and they may not know it

It all came from my mother who never loses but wins

Wins are associated with those who have and give Love

Love Exist

LOVE EXIST

Write a song of love and have someone else sings it

It will be heard by all but not all will be able to love

Love will next allow more participants to join the club

Club of those who have plenty of floating love

Love and dance with others the song of love

Love will make it happen if not today then on another

Another one will approach you soon with Love

Love Exist

No regrets, doubts, shame, or fear

Fear not even if you decided not to love. Fear not at all

All those who hate must fear because hate will return back

Back in the day, it can be proved to you. Hate does not work

Work hard to empty your heart from hate and replace love

Love is the best medicine. It is quick and magic

Magic river full of unlimited Love

Love Exist

Learn to love like 1, 2, 3 or A, B, C. sing it like kids

Kids love to love and laugh

Laugh, smile, and live like kids

Kids do exist at all time and therefore love

Love is inside each one of us. Your childhood proofs it

It can be done now as it was happening before

Before you were born you were born for Love

Love Exist

With modern technology, there are many new codes

Codes make our life faster and easier to live and to love

Love and never stop even if some do

Do spread the word, the act, the behavior, and the hope

Hope and pray for a better world inside you

You are not alone. Believe it

It is your faith that tells you to Love

Love Exist

My neighbor wonders about my grandmother's age

Age of my grandmother is counterclockwise. She gets younger

Younger you are with all that you do

Do everything with love and you will never get old

Old you are who has not tried to be kind

Kind is my grandmother even to herself

Herself is last because she provides Love

Love Exist

The war began and my brother volunteered

Volunteered to stand by those who have volunteered

Volunteered to give up his life among other volunteers

Volunteers love their country. They willing to give up their lives

Lives are the price to free the land of their homes

Homes celebrates the love of their sons

Sons are the men of Love

Love Exist

My parents were gone early. I was raised among strangers

Strangers threw me in the pit

The pit was dark and very deep

Deep in depression, despair, misery, and despair

Despair is the norm of my life now, then, and the future

Future and life are gone with my parents

Parents are the source of life and Love

Love Exist

Calm down all the times if possible

Possible to gain almost everything if you have control

Control comes from self-control and self-esteem

Self-esteem is within

Within each one of us is love which gives you confidence

Confidence is the compass of your life

Life begins and ends with Love

Love Exist

LOVE EXIST

A daughter flew to another country for vacation and never returned

Returned to her creator with the rest of the crew members

Members of family members mourn for the lost

Lost forever and everything is dark today

Today may be the new beginning for some

Some are finally freed from the bodily bondage

Bondage of the worldly matters and burdens

Burdens do not belong anymore for those who had Love

Love Exist

Every day I hear the same song over and over

Over the years the same song carries over my daily life

Life is not repeated but the same song

Song of love to love those who are here and over there

There must be lights somewhere every single day

Day after another I am getting closer to those who had Love

Love Exist

Love does not require you to do anything but act

Act and your actions will be the seeds of the trees of love

Love grows and grows to become trees to nest humans and birds

Birds are signs for life to those who lost hope in life

Life for some may have a beginning without an end

End the resting time. It is time to go to work

Work with everyone possible to plant more trees of Love

Love Exist

Human changes guaranteed but climate changes

Changes may take longer times but they will

Will you be able to be changed? If not, then what?

What are other options for not changing? Limited to none

None of what you have now will be the same if you chose to

To you are some possibilities. Chose one

One of the possibilities is to Love

Love Exist

Best of luck to you dear friend

Friend of the past is no longer a friend of today or tomorrow

Tomorrow I will still remember you

You were part of me. I cannot tear myself apart

Apart are the eyes not the heart

Heart beats to love. Love everyone

Everyone is loved by me because I have it. Love

Love Exist

I am thirteen years old born on the 13th of the month

The month of the 13th does not exist

Exist one day before or after is not ideal or better

Better days are short and less than thirteen

Thirteen may not be your favorite but it is mine

Mine is everything God has made

Made for honor and Love

Love Exist

Four letters make the word LOVE

Love is deep. The world's letters cannot fulfill it

It is inside you and each one of us. Use it

It may solve all your problems or be the solution to the major

Major problem does not exist anymore

Any more to come will come and will pass away

Away from you all your problems if you allow Love

Love Exist

Little pieces together and united are all of you

You have all these and those pieces

Pieces are inside and outside of you. The inside is the most

Most of them are very similar to others but a few

Few are unique to you only

Only you may figure some of them out

Out there trying to give out some Love

Love Exist

LOVE EXIST

Times of tribulations come and go

Go find a place of comfort and worry-free

Free, calm, and relax to better thinking

Thinking less and doing more

More or less maybe soon. It is all up to the circumstances

Circumstances for all humans without any exceptions

Exceptions are temporary because things repeat

Repeat not your mistakes but your Love

Love Exist

Gather your friends and have a good time

Time with friends is countless and endless

Endless is the love between each one of you

You take care of this friendship with love and care

Care about your friends and if they do not you still do

Do not stop to support your friend with Love

Love Exist

You have more qualifications than you think

Think of what you have. Master it to gain what you do not have

Have the strength to resist, repel, and prevent all its obstacles

Obstacles exist to power you for success

Success comes in a special form to those who love

Love and celebrate others' successes

Successes are plenty especially yours

Yours are not yours but for others' to celebrate with Love

Love Exist

Touch the fur of your pet with gentleness to reach its heart

Heart of your pet is alive for your love

Love your pet and you gain the whole life

Life of your pet is short like yours

Yours are all the laughs with him or her

Her children will have a new life with you in Love

Love Exist

LOVE EXIST

Feeding an ant with love is better than feeding an elephant without

Without love, everything vanishes and become ashes

Ashes do not hear, smell, touch, see, or smell

Smell the scent of your deeds

Deeds are who you are

Are you sharing your life with others?

Others are not here always. Act with Love

Love Exist

I have lived with someone who loves me but never said the word

The word means nothing if all the acts show his or her love

Love is there if you need anything

Anything can be seen through your love

Love to be

Be there to inspire the universe

The universe needs every individual's Love

Love Exist

Unsecure and polluted environments are the inhabitants of many

Many are forsaking without looking back

Back in days, it was so much different

Different times the different climate

Climate needs your love interference. Each one has a role

A role of the simple one may be the greatest of all

All we need is some Love

Love Exist

Last night for the first time I had a dinner

Dinner is a pleasure for many people

People somewhere see food in others' hands, not theirs

Theirs is very little for very long time

Time has passed. Things are the same. No changes

Changes, please

Please remember me because I do exist like Love

Love Exist

Compete and race to give love for your riches

Riches endure for you and your family

Family full of riches

Riches have many paths. Best is through love

Love is better than diamond and anything else

Else you may excuse anything but God and love

Love is God and God is Love

Love Exist

A lucky day never knocked on my door

Door of happiness is my dream

Dream to wake up from sleep to love

Love those who are indoors and outdoors

Outdoors and indoors have unlimited doors

Doors of the same lock and same key

Key of Love

Love Exist

You probably do not remember me but I do

Do I remember how I was reborn because of your kindness?

Kindness has saved my entire family

Family members are all praying for you

You have shown us the existence of kindness

Kindness comes out of a loving person

Person among us has Love

Love Exist

Born and raised in a church the house of God

God blesses his own house. The house of love

Love is everywhere even in your house

House of love may be yours if you decide to

To you and your family the light of love

Love in a poor house is better than a mansion or a palace without

Without love simple things are impossible. Love

Love Exist

LOVE EXIST

Love makes you tear sometimes. Tears of happiness

Happiness is when everyone around you loves you

You do not have to do miracles. Just love and act

Act and it will be done

Done of depressed tears but happy tears

Tears clean the eyes and establish sight

Sight and clear vision you may obtain with Love

Love Exist

Buy two bars of candy. One for you and one for someone

Someone may not appreciate your gift today but tomorrow

Tomorrow your reward is paid if not to you, then to your children

Children and their children to come and maybe forever

Forever love lasts and never stops its rewards

Rewards are included in the eternal life as well

Well, you know how it works now. Live to Love

Love Exist

There are no specific instructions to follow

Follow your heart because it was created to love

Love your life and everything in it

It happens once. I mean your life. Make it abundantly full of love

Love will make you live your life younger forever

Forever you will live because those who love do not die

Die from every evil thought and replace it with Love

Love Exist

Love exists even where life does not exist such as outer space

Space is made out of love. God created it by love and for love

Love exists in the full universe. There is no place without love

Love may be taken away from some places if their owners choose

Choose not to be in a place where there is no love. Run away

Away you must be to enjoy your life and to have success

Success takes place where love takes place. Place Love

Love Exist

LOVE EXIST

Some supplements of love are with children

Children are sorts of love. Play with them and realize

Realize the purity of loves and laughs

Laughs allow hearts to beat for joy

Joy is your daughter's first name and your life

Life with children is like Heaven on earth

Earth and Heaven are not the same but with Love

Love Exist

Hurry up the train is leaving the platform

The platform only receives passengers and does not provide them

Them are gone. They cannot take the train to come back

Back in time, there was a chance to repent and change but not now

Now is judgment. It all depends on your deeds while on the train

The train will stop soon completely and everyone will get out

Out there somewhere some people wish they did give Love

Love Exist

The best example of the love of all times is The Cross

The Cross of Our Lord Jesus Christ

Christ has saved all Humans from Hades to Heaven

Heaven is now open and ready to receive you

You follow the commandments with love and you enter

Enter the eternity where no one ever able to describe

Describe if you can what you can do with Love

Love Exist

I was gifted with cancer which almost ate my whole body

Body was about to be decomposed soon until he came

Came to give me his love and my hope

Hope to survive with him. I did it

It was done through his love injections into my blood vessels

Vessels full of his love

Love saved my life. Thanks to his Love

Love Exist

About the Author

Isaac Nash was born and raised in Egypt as a Coptic Orthodox Christian. He lives in the U.S.A with his wife and his three children. His first book "THE HEROK" was published in March 2021 followed by his second book "GOD EXIST" in May 2021. This book "LOVE EXIST" is part of the EXIST series.

The author can be reached at heroknash@gmail.com